WHAT TO DO IF AN ELEPHANT STANDS ON YOUR FOOT

by Michelle Robinson

pictures by Peter H. Reynolds

PUFFIN

If an elephant stands on your foot, keep calm.

Panicking will only startle it.

OOOWWW!!!

Never mind, these things happen.

In the event of startling an elephant, you will probably feel like running away, rather quickly.

Try not to!
Running may
attract tigers.

Told you so.

SHHH! Once a tiger has spotted you,

you MUST stay silent!

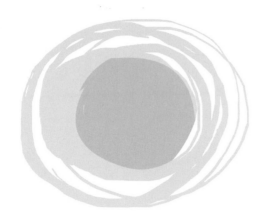

The slightest sound,
such as a sneeze . . .

Oh dear.

As I was saying, make the slightest
sound and rhinoceroses will hear you.

If a rhinoceros has heard you,
whatever you do . . .

... DO **NOT** BE TEMPTED
TO CLIMB A TREE.

Oh, for goodness' sake!
Go ahead then, if you must –
but don't say I didn't warn you!

See? Snakes live in trees, and they do NOT take kindly to visitors.

Having found yourself in a snakes' tree, take a few deep breaths and steady yourself.

That's it. Now, sit tight and try not to make any sudden movements.

Like that one. You ninny!

Sudden movements do NOT
go unnoticed by crocodiles!
Everyone knows that!

Honestly, you're hopeless!

If you've been noticed by a crocodile,
don't expect me to help you.

Oh, all right then,
since you asked so nicely.

Wave your arms around
and shout for help!

Is it working?

Yes!

Here come the monkeys!

Of course, now that the monkeys have arrived, there's only one thing to do . . .

...GO NUTS!

Jump up and down!
Run around and around!

Sing and shout and dance and swing!

Have a banana!

And finally, before you return
to your nice, safe home . . .

. . . remember your manners!
Thank the monkeys for rescuing you,

and don't forget to apologize to the elephant.

Just be careful not to . . . .

For Isabelle Kaitlyn from Auntie Mash – M.R.

To Janet Reynolds, who always seems to know what to do! – P.H.R.

PUFFIN BOOKS

Published by the Penguin Group: London, New York,

Australia, Canada, India, Ireland, New Zealand and South Africa

Penguin Books Ltd, Registered Offices: 80 Strand, London WC2R 0RL, England

puffinbooks.com

First published in the USA by Dial Books, an imprint of Penguin Group (USA) Inc., 2012

Published in Great Britain by Puffin Books 2012

Text copyright © Michelle Robinson, 2012

Illustrations copyright © Peter H. Reynolds, 2012

The moral right of the author and illustrator has been asserted

All rights reserved

Made and printed in China

ISBN: 978–0–141–32715–0

001 – 10 9 8 7 6 5 4 3 2 1